~ *Kidnapped* ~

BULLSEYE STEP INTO CLASSICS™

Kidnapped

By Robert Louis Stevenson
Adapted by Lisa Norby

Bullseye Step into Classics™

Random House 🏠 New York

A BULLSEYE BOOK PUBLISHED BY RANDOM HOUSE, INC.
Text copyright © 1994 by Random House, Inc.
Cover illustration copyright © 1994 by Dan Andreasen.

Library of Congress Cataloging-in-Publication Data:
Norby, Lisa. Kidnapped / by Robert Louis Stevenson ; adapted by Lisa Norby.
p. cm. — (Bullseye step into classics)
SUMMARY: After being kidnapped by his villainous uncle, seventeen-year-old
David Balfour escapes and becomes involved in the struggle of the Scottish
highlanders under English rule.
ISBN: 0-679-85091-0
[1. Scotland—History—18th century—Fiction. 2. Adventure and adventurers—
Fiction.] I. Stevenson, Robert Louis, 1850-1894. Kidnapped. II. Title.
III. Series.
PZ7.N7752Ki 1994 [Fic]—dc20 93-4609

Cover design by Fabia Wargin Design and Creative Media Applications, Inc.

Manufactured in the United States of America 10 9 8 7 6 5 4 3

Contents

~ Kidnapped ~

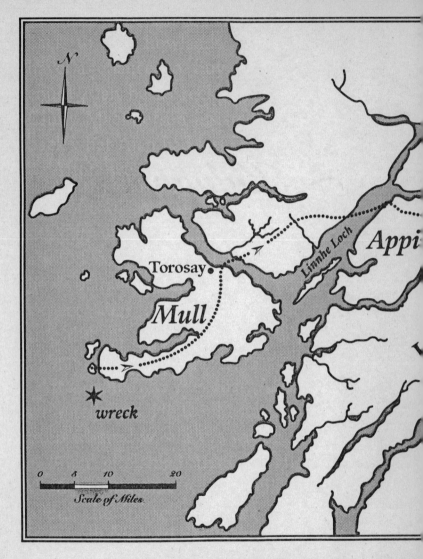

N

Torosay

Mull

Appi

Linnhe Loch

wreck

0   5   10   20
Scale of Miles

ROUTE OF THE BRIG *COVENANT*

DAVID BALFOUR'S

Atlantic
Ocean

Cape Wrath

North
Sea

HIGHLANDS

Mull

LOWLANDS

Queen's
Ferry Edinburgh

SCOTLAND

ENGLAND

GHLANDS

LOWLANDS

Queen's Ferry

AROUND SCOTLAND &
PATH THROUGH THE HIGHLANDS

1

I Leave Home

I will begin the story of my adventures with a certain morning in June of the year 1751. That was the day I left my father's house for the last time. The hills around my little Scottish village were hidden by fog. But as I went down the road, the sun came out. I hoped the change was a good sign.

Soon I reached the house of old Mr. Campbell, the parson. Mr. Campbell himself was waiting by the garden gate. He offered to walk with me a way to see me off.

"Are you sorry to be leaving Essendean?" he asked.

"Sir," I said, "Essendean is a good place. But now that my mother and father are both dead, I must seek my fortune."

"Very well, Davie," said Mr. Campbell. "Then I will tell your fortune as far as I know it. After your mother died and your father fell ill, he gave me this letter. 'As soon as I am gone,' he told me, 'put this letter in my boy's hand. Then send him to the house of Shaws, near Cramond. That is where I come from.'"

"The house of Shaws!" I cried. Everyone knew this was a gentleman's estate. "What did my father have to do with the house of Shaws?"

"Who can be sure?" Mr. Campbell

said. "Your father was better educated than the usual country schoolteacher."

My father's letter was addressed to Ebenezer Balfour, Esquire, of Shaws. Balfour was my last name, too.

My heart was beating hard. I was just seventeen, the son of a poor man. Suddenly, I saw myself becoming rich.

"Mr. Campbell," I said. "If you were in my shoes, would you go?"

"Oh, surely," said he. "Cramond is near Edinburgh. A young lad like you could walk there in two days."

It was now time for us to part. But Mr. Campbell could not let me go without giving me some good advice. He took a seat on a large rock. Then he placed his handkerchief over his hat to keep the sun out of his eyes.

"Now, Davie, don't forget to say your prayers," he began.

After he had covered the subject of religion, Mr. Campbell went on to talk about manners. "Remember," he said, "Shaws is a rich man's house. Don't shame us."

Mr. Campbell put his arms around me and hugged me hard. His face was all twisted up in his effort to keep from crying. Some boys would have laughed. Instead, I felt guilty. The truth was, I was happy to be getting away from this quiet country village. Nothing exciting ever happened here.

2

The Gloomy
House of Shaws

Before noon the next day, I came to the top of a great hill. In the distance I could see the city of Edinburgh, covered with a blanket of smoke. Beyond lay the sea.

A shepherd gave me directions to Cramond. Soon I began asking the way to Shaws. But when I mentioned the name of the house, people looked surprised. At first, I thought they were wondering why a poor boy like me wanted to see the rich Mr. Balfour. Then I began to think that there must be something strange about the house itself.

Along came a man driving a heavy farm cart. He had an honest face, so I decided to question him.

"Do you know of the folk who live at the house of Shaws?" I asked.

"Folk? There are none. At least not what I call folk," he said.

Now I was confused. "What about the lord of the manor, Ebenezer Balfour?"

"Oh, aye." He peered down at me from his cart. "It's none of my business, but you seem a decent lad. Take my advice. Stay away from Mr. Balfour and the house of Shaws."

So much for my dreams. I thought

about turning back right then. But I had walked for two days to get this far. I decided to go on.

Around sundown, I passed a stout, sour-looking woman. When I asked her my usual question, she pointed to a big building in the next valley. The country-side all around it looked pleasant. The fields were planted with crops. But the house itself appeared to be in ruins.

"That is the house of Shaws!" cried the woman in a weird singsong voice. "Blood built it. Blood stopped the building of it. Blood shall bring it down."

The woman turned with a skip and was gone. I stood where I was, my hair on end. In those days I still believed in witches.

The closer I came to Shaws, the gloomier it seemed. The upper floors in one wing of the house were unfinished. One whole wall was missing. Elsewhere in the wing, the windows were gaping holes. Bats flew in and out.

In the main part of the house, the first-floor windows were narrow and high off the ground. The light from a small fire shone through several of them. I could hear someone coughing inside. Gathering my courage, I raised my hand and knocked once on the door.

Silence.

I knocked again.

Whoever was in the house kept deadly still.

I wanted to give up and run away, but anger got the better of me. I pounded on the door and kicked at it, shouting for Mr. Balfour.

At last I heard a dry cough right above

my head. I looked up and saw a man in a nightcap, leaning out of a window. He was holding a long gun, the old-fashioned kind called a blunderbuss.

"It's loaded," warned the old man.

"I have come here with a letter," I said, "for Mr. Ebenezer Balfour. Is he here?"

"Put it down on the doorstep and be off with ye."

"I will do no such thing," I answered. "It is a letter of introduction."

"And who might you be?" the old man asked.

"David Balfour," said I.

At this, the man started to shake. "What! Is your father dead?" he asked.

This surprised me so much that I didn't answer.

"Aye, he'll be dead, no doubt,' the man said. "That's what brings you to the door."

He paused, then finally said, "I'll let you in."

With a great rattling of chains and bolts, the door swung open. The man showed me into the kitchen. It was the barest room I had ever seen. The only furniture was a rough table and a few locked chests in the corner.

By the light of the fire, I had a better look at the man. He was a small, stoop-shouldered person who wore an old nightshirt over his ragged clothes. It had been days since he last shaved. He could have been fifty years old. Or seventy. It was impossible to tell. I decided that he must be a servant, hired to keep watch over the house.

"Are ye hungry?" he asked. He pointed to a bowl of porridge on the table. "Ye can have that."

I said I couldn't eat his own dinner.

"Oh, I'll do fine without it," he said. "Now let's see the letter."

"It's for Mr. Balfour, not for you," I said.

"And who do you think I am?" he said. "Give me Alexander's letter."

"How do you know my father's name?" I cried.

"It would be strange if I didn't. He was my born brother. And as little as you may like me, Davie, I am your uncle."

If I had been a few years younger, I would have burst into tears. Tired and disappointed, I sat down at the table and began to eat the porridge.

My uncle turned the letter over in his hands. "Why did you come here? I suppose you expect me to help you."

"Yes, that is so," I said. "But I am no

beggar!" I added. "I have friends who will look out for me."

"Hoot-toot!" cried Uncle Ebenezer. "Don't fly up at me. We'll get along yet." And seeing that I was not going to finish the porridge, he grabbed my spoon and began gobbling it up.

While he ate, my uncle questioned me. He wanted to know if my father ever talked about him. When I said no, he seemed pleased.

Uncle Ebenezer led me up a flight of stairs to a bedroom where I could spend the night. He had no lamp, not even a candle. The room was so dark I couldn't find the bed. But when I asked for a light, Uncle refused.

"Hoot-toot! Hoot-toot!" he said. "I don't hold with lights in the house. I'm too afraid of fire."

With that, he left, pulling the door shut behind him. I heard the sound of the key turning, locking me in.

The bed, when I finally found it, was damp and moldy smelling. So I lay down on the floor and wrapped myself in my plaid cape. And that is how I finally fell asleep.

3

The Dark Tower

At the first peep of day, I opened my eyes. I found myself in a large room. It must have been a very pleasant place ten or twenty years ago. But since then dirt, mice, and spiders had taken over. I pounded on the door until my uncle came and let me out.

Breakfast was more porridge, grayish and watery. After Uncle had finished eating, he took a clay pipe and some tobacco out of a locked drawer. While he smoked, he began to question me.

"Who are these friends of yours?" he wanted to know.

The truth was, I had just been bragging. Old Parson Campbell was the only person in my village who had shown any interest in me. But I didn't trust my uncle. I thought it would be a bad idea to let him know that I was all alone in the world. So I told him that several gentlemen named Campbell were looking out for me.

"Well, Davie," said Uncle, "I wouldn't want the Campbells to think badly of the Balfours. I will do right by you yet. But don't you be telling anyone news of this house. No letters or messages to anyone, mind you. Or else I'll show you the door."

"I have my pride, too," I said. "It wasn't my idea to come here. If I'm not welcome, I will leave."

"Nay, nay, stay. I am not a magician. I can't find a fortune for you in the bottom of a porridge bowl. But give me time." He shot me a crafty look. "What's mine is yours, laddie. And what's yours is mine."

"Uncle Ebenezer," I said, "what is going on? You clearly don't like me. Yet you keep urging me to stay."

"Nay, nay," he repeated. "I like you fine. For the honor of the house, I can't let you leave the way you came."

Then he began to talk about the noble history of the Balfours. He explained that it was his father's idea to enlarge the house. He himself had put a stop to the work because it was a waste of money.

I spent the rest of the day looking

around the house. The room next to the kitchen held a large number of books. In one of them I found a few words in my father's handwriting: "To my brother Ebenezer on his fifth birthday."

This puzzled me. Since Ebenezer had inherited the house, he must be the older brother. That meant my father would have been younger than five when he wrote this. For his age, he certainly had fine, clear handwriting!

Dinner that evening was another bowl of porridge. My mind was still on the book I had found.

"Tell me, Uncle," I said. "Was my father very young when he learned to read and write?"

For some reason, my question made Uncle nervous. He dropped his spoon and grabbed me by the arm. "Why do you ask that?" he wanted to know.

"Take your hand off me," I ordered. "This is no way to behave."

Was my uncle insane? Or was there another reason for his strange behavior? If my father was the older brother, then the house had been rightfully his. Now it should be mine.

Uncle and I eyed each other warily, like a cat and a mouse. At last he said, "Davie, I just remembered. There is a wee bit of gold that I promised to you before you were born. Rather, I promised it to your father. I have been keeping it all these years. It comes to a handsome sum—forty pounds in English money."

Uncle Ebenezer didn't want me to see where he kept his money. He sent me out into the cold, and I waited until he called me back in. When I returned, he counted out almost forty pounds in gold coins. He couldn't bear to part with any more.

I thanked him politely. But I knew it was a trick. The old miser would never give me so much gold for no reason. I was waiting to hear what would come next.

My uncle then explained that all he wanted in return was a little help with the house and garden. This sounded reasonable. I almost felt guilty for suspecting him.

"I'll do what I can," I promised.

"Well then, let's begin," he said. He reached into his pocket and pulled out a rusty key. "This is the key to the tower at the far end of the house. That part of the house was never finished. You can only get into the tower from outdoors. Climb the stairs and bring me the chest that is at the top. There are papers in it."

"Can I take a light with me?" I asked.

"No," he answered. "I told you. No lights in my house."

"Very well, sir," said I. "Are the stairs good?"

"The stairs are grand," said he. "There is no railing. But the stairs are solid."

I went out into the night. There was no moon. The wind was howling in the distance. I felt my way along the wall of the house until I came to the tower door.

Inside the tower it was so dark that I could hardly breathe. The stairs were steep, but they were made of stone. Keeping close to the wall, I began to climb.

The house of Shaws was a full five stories high, not counting the attics. As I made my way up the stairs, the air felt much less stuffy. Suddenly there came a flash of summer lightning. And I saw why the air was fresher. The lightning shone in through big gaps in the stone walls.

While the light lasted, I saw that the

steps were not all of the same length. The one I was standing on was very narrow. My foot was only a few inches from the open edge!

I couldn't let Uncle know he had scared me. I kept on climbing. But I felt every step with my hands before I set my weight on it. Above me, I could hear a great stirring of bats.

The tower was square, and at each corner there was a large stone landing. I was just coming to one of these landings when my hand slipped over the forward edge. It found nothing but emptiness beyond. Now I knew my uncle had sent me up into the tower to die.

I turned around and began feeling my way downward. As I reached the bottom of the stairs there was another flash of lightning, followed by a great tow-row of thunder. I caught a glimpse of Uncle standing outside the kitchen door. Maybe he thought the thunder was the sound of me falling to my death. Maybe he thought it was God's judgment on him. He shook with fright and disappeared inside.

When I reached the kitchen, I found Uncle seated at the table with his back to me. He was drinking brandy right from the bottle. I tiptoed up behind him and clapped my hands down on his shoulders. "Ah!" I cried.

Uncle gave a weak bleat like a sheep's and fell over. For a minute, I was afraid he was dead. But he had only fainted from fright. Little by little, he began to stir.

"Are ye alive?" he croaked. "Are ye alive?"

"That I am," I told him. "No thanks to you."

I felt a little sorry for him, but I meant to hear the truth. Why had he been so afraid when I asked about my father's age?

"I'll tell you in the morning," he said. "Sure as death, I will."

Uncle was so weak that I had no choice. I would have to wait for his explanation. But I locked him in his room for the night.

Then I returned to the kitchen. I made a big fire in the fireplace, the biggest fire seen in that house for many a year. And curling up on the wooden chests, I fell fast asleep.

4

I Am Kidnapped

The next morning, I went out to the stream that ran near the house and took a dip. Then I sat down to think things over. I had no doubt that my uncle would kill me if he could. But surely I was clever enough to get the better of an old man like him!

When I returned to the house, I let Uncle Ebenezer out of his bedroom.

"Well, sir," I said. "You took me for a stupid country boy, a Johnny Raw. I took you for a good man. We were both wrong. Why did you try to end my life?"

Before I could force my uncle to talk, there came a knocking on the door. When I answered it, I found a half-grown boy, a few years younger than me. He was dressed like a sailor. As soon as he saw me, he did a few steps of the jaunty sailor's dance called the hornpipe.

"I have a letter from old Heasy-oasy to Mr. Bellflower," said the boy. "And I say, mate, I am very hungry."

I invited the lad inside. While he was finishing the leftovers of my own breakfast, Uncle read the letter.

"You see," said my uncle, showing the letter to me. "I have business with this man Hoseason, who is the captain of the trading ship *Covenant*. He is about to sail for the New World. Today is my last chance to see him.

"Walk with me over to Queen's Ferry, where his ship lies," Uncle added. "Then you can meet with my lawyer, Mr. Rankeillor. He is a well-respected man, and he knew your father. He will answer all your questions. You wouldn't believe what I told you anyway."

I thought and thought. I couldn't see anything wrong with this plan. Queen's Ferry was a busy place. I would be safer there than alone with Uncle at Shaws. Besides, I longed to get a good look at the big sailing ships in the harbor. I would take the gold that Uncle had given me. Perhaps this man Rankeillor could keep it safe.

So the three of us started out for

Queen's Ferry. Uncle Ebenezer didn't say a word the whole way. I passed the time oy talking to the cabin boy. His name was Ransome. He showed me his tattoos and told stories about the wild things that he had done. But even though he swore horribly, he sounded like a silly schoolboy.

Ransome told me what a wonderful man Captain Heasy-oasy was. (Heasy-oasy, I figured out, was his way of saying the name Hoseason.) But he said the captain had one fault. "He's no seaman. It's the first mate, Mr. Shuan, who navigates. He's the finest pilot in the trade. Only he drinks."

When Mr. Shuan got drunk, Ransome added, he turned into a bully. The cabin boy pulled down his sock. There was an ugly gash on his leg where Mr. Shuan had cut him. Then he showed me a knife. "Let him try to do me again!" he boasted. "I dare him to."

Ransome's stories made my blood run cold. If sea and wind didn't kill the boy, the cruel Mr. Shuan would.

"Can't you find some honest life ashore?" I asked.

"Oh no," said Ransome with a wink. "They would make me learn a trade."

I could see that he would rather put up with danger and bullies than work at a regular job on land.

"Besides, there's worse off than me," he added. And he began to tell me stories of criminals who were sentenced to be shipped to North America as slaves. Worse, sometimes innocent people were kidnapped and sent off to the same fate. Even children!

Soon we reached Queen's Ferry. The *Covenant* lay at anchor about half a mile away. On board there was a great hustle and bustle as the sailors got the ship ready to sail. Uncle went into the Hawes Inn to meet with the captain. I waited outside. Ransome showed me the ship's boat tied up at the pier.

Ransome's stories of kidnappings had frightened me. "No power on earth could get me to set foot on that ship," I said.

But then Captain Hoseason came down to the pier with my uncle. The captain was a tall, dark, serious-looking man. He spoke to me as an equal, though I was only a lad.

"Sir," said he in a fine deep voice, "perhaps you will come aboard my brig for half an hour. Afterwards the ship's boat will return you and your uncle to town, near Mr. Rankeillor's house."

Then the captain leaned down and whispered in my ear. "The old man means you harm. Come aboard so I can have a word with you about him."

As he spoke, Captain Hoseason took my arm and helped me into the boat. In spite of everything, I longed to visit the *Covenant*. And the captain's manner made me think that I had found a friend. What a fool I was!

When we pulled up beside the ship, the sailors dropped a rope to lift us onto the deck. A little dizzy from the ride, I took in all the sights on board.

Suddenly it struck me that something was wrong. Uncle Ebenezer had been in the boat with us, but I didn't see him on deck.

I knew I was lost. Sure enough, when I ran to the rail, I saw the ship's boat heading back for town. Uncle was sitting in the rear. He looked up at me with a face full of cruelty and terror.

That face was the last thing I saw. I felt strong hands pulling at me. Then a thunderbolt seemed to strike me, and I fell to the deck.

5

* *

A Prisoner at Sea

I came to in the darkness. My feet and hands were tied. My body ached. My ears were filled with the roar of rushing water. The whole world heaved up and down. There were rats all around me. Their feet went pitter-patter on the wooden floor. Every so often, one would dash across my face.

I was in the cargo hold of the ship. We must have put out to sea and run into a great storm. I could hear the wind lashing at the sails.

Lying in that foul place, I caught a fever. I don't know how much time passed. Night and day were the same in the dark. I fell asleep.

The next thing I knew, I was awakened by the light of a lantern. A small man with green eyes and fair hair was peering down at me. I soon learned this was Mr. Riach, the second mate.

"Well," he said, "how goes it?"

I answered with a sob.

He felt my forehead. Then he washed the cut on my head and gave me a drink of water.

The next time Mr. Riach visited me, he brought Captain Hoseason.

"See for yourself, sir," he said. "The boy is burning up. I want him moved to the forecastle. If you don't move him, you are no better than a paid murderer."

"What kind of talk is that!" the captain cried. "I am a hard man. But murder!"

At last the captain gave in. I was moved to a bunk in the crew's quarters. I lay there for days and got back my health. The sailors were a rough lot, but they were kind to me. They even returned my money. They had stolen it from my pockets before I was thrown in the hold.

The sailors told me that Ransome's stories were true. Scottish people were being kidnapped into slavery. And I was one of them. The *Covenant* was bound for the Carolinas, where the captain planned to sell me to a plantation owner. No doubt my uncle had made a bargain with Hoseason to get me out of his way.

I soon learned that Ransome's stories

about the *Covenant*'s first mate were also true. Mr. Shuan was a good man until he got drunk. Then he turned mean and attacked the boy.

Mr. Riach, on the other hand, became kinder the drunker he got. But Riach had started giving Ransome rum to drink. Maybe he meant well. But it was sad to see the cabin boy drunk and talking nonsense. A few of the sailors laughed. But most shook their heads. Maybe they were thinking of their own children, whom they hadn't seen in years.

One night about midnight, a sailor came into the forecastle bringing bad news. "Shuan has done for him at last," he whispered. I knew right away that something had happened to Ransome.

Soon, Captain Hoseason came down the ladder. "You are moving into the roundhouse," he told me. "We need you to serve as cabin boy."

As he spoke, two sailors came in carrying Ransome in their arms. His poor face was as white as wax. His mouth was fixed in a dreadful smile.

I did as I was told. The roundhouse was where the captain and the two mates, Shuan and Riach, ate and slept. It was above deck, and it had two little windows and a skylight. I was grateful for the chance to see the sky.

My duties were light, but the mood in the roundhouse was grim. Captain Hoseason was furious with Mr. Shuan for killing Ransome. He and Mr. Riach made up their minds that no one back in port would ever know the truth. They agreed to say that Ransome had fallen overboard.

The shock of what he had done soon drove Mr. Shuan out of his mind. At times I caught him staring at me strangely. "Who are you?" he once asked. "Wasn't there another boy?" I should have hated him, but I couldn't help feeling pity.

Bad luck and stormy weather had followed the *Covenant* from the beginning of her voyage. It took us nine days to reach Cape Wrath, the northern tip of Scotland. At last we rounded the cape. Then we began to sail south, along the rocky western coast.

On the afternoon of the tenth day, a thick fog came down. The sailors hung over the rail, watching out for rocks below the surface of the water.

About ten at night I was serving dinner in the roundhouse. Suddenly the ship struck something. We all ran out on deck. We had hit a smaller boat, slicing it in half. All the men on board but one had gone to the bottom.

That one man had been sitting in the rear of the boat. When the crash came, he was thrown up into the air. He managed to catch hold of the *Covenant*'s bowsprit, the strong pole that thrusts forward at the front of the ship. He was very lucky to be alive. But when he was shown into the roundhouse, he looked as cool as could be.

The man was small but well built. His sunburned face was covered with freckles and pitted with scars. His eyes had a kind of dancing madness in them. When he took off his coat, I saw that he carried a pair of silver pistols and a long sword. In all, I thought he was the sort of man I would rather have as a friend than an enemy.

The stranger's clothes were as fine as his manners. His hat had feathers on it. Under his heavy overcoat he wore a red vest, black velvet knee pants, and a blue coat trimmed with silver buttons and lace.

Captain Hoseason studied the little man's clothes with interest. "There are many fine coats in France," he said.

The stranger's hands went for his pistols. "Are ye of the honest party?" he demanded.

"I am a true-blue Protestant," the captain answered. "But for all that, I can be sorry to see another man with his back to the wall."

I knew that by the "honest party" the stranger meant the followers of the old

Catholic ruling family, the Stuarts. The last Stuart king had been driven out of England over sixty years ago. But his grandson lived in France, plotting to get the throne back. And many in the northern part of Scotland, the mountain-filled Highlands, were still loyal to him.

Just six years ago, a party of Stuart rebels had landed in Scotland. They raised an army of Highlanders and marched on London. The rebels were beaten. But they would never admit their cause was lost.

The stranger now told the captain he was with the rebels. He was a smuggler, taking money raised in the Highlands to the Stuart plotters in France.

This spry little man with his fancy clothes was an outlaw. If he was caught, he would surely hang. I couldn't help staring at him. He had the look of a man who faced danger every day of his life. What adventures he must have had!

I was even more amazed when the stranger opened his coat and took off a money belt filled with gold coins. He offered the captain a rich reward to take him safely to France.

Captain Hoseason refused. The voyage to France would be too risky. But for a price, he was willing to put him ashore in Scotland.

"I'll give you thirty coins to set me down here on the coast," the little man said. "Sixty if you return me to Linnhe Loch, where my friends will be nearby."

"I see," said Captain Hoseason. "Sixty it is." And he went outside.

I served the stranger his supper, and he asked me for a drink of rum. All the spirits were kept in a locked cupboard. So I went out on deck to get the key from the captain. I found him whispering with Mr. Riach and Mr. Shuan.

"Davie," the captain said to me, "that wild Highlander is a danger to us all. Our guns are in that cupboard. You can fetch a few pistols for us. If we try to get them, he will suspect that he is in danger.

"Help us," Hoseason added, "and you shall have your share of the gold."

Now the plot was clear to me. The captain and the mates were going to kill the stranger and take his money. But I was just a boy. What was I to do?

6

The Fight in
the Roundhouse

Back in the roundhouse, the stranger was finishing his supper. He had no idea that his life was in danger. All at once, my mind was made up. No matter what happened, I had to warn him.

"They are all murderers here," I cried out. "They killed a boy already. Now it's you!"

The stranger leaped to his feet. "Aye, but they haven't got me yet. I will fight them all! Will you stand with me?"

My chest felt tight. My mouth was dry. How could two of us take on the whole crew? Still, I couldn't side with the men who murdered poor Ransome. "I am with you," I promised him.

Quickly, we opened the cupboard. I loaded all the pistols. While I worked, the stranger introduced himself. "I am a Stewart, and they call me Alan Breck," he said.

Stewart was a well-known name. It was another way of spelling Stuart, the name of the former king. Alan was a distant relative of the old royal family.

Alan saw me frown. "And what about you? Are you for the Stuarts? Or are you a Whig?" he asked.

The Whigs were the party loyal to King George. I was a Whig all the way. But this did not seem like a good time to pick a quarrel. "In between," I said.

Alan laughed. "Well, Mr. In-between, here is our plan. I will hold them off at the main door. You must guard my back."

This was a tall order. The roundhouse had a rear door and a glass skylight. There were also the two windows, big enough to stick a gun through.

Alan told me to take the pistols and climb onto one of the bunks. He stood at the main door, a sword in one hand and a dagger in the other.

"How many are against us?" he asked.

"Fifteen," I said.

Alan whistled. "Well, that can't be helped."

Out on deck, the captain had begun to

get suspicious. Suddenly, he stuck his face in the open door of the roundhouse. He saw at once that I was planning to stand with Alan.

"I won't forgive this, David," the captain said to me.

Soon I could hear him passing out swords to the crew. My heart was beating like a bird's. Then the battle began. Mr. Shuan led the main charge at the open doorway. He slashed at Alan with his sword. Alan slashed back.

I had no time to watch the duel. Through the window by my post, I saw five sailors come running with a long pole. They were getting ready to break the rear door down.

I had never fired a pistol in my life. Now I had no choice. I leaned out the window and took aim. "Take that!" I shouted. I shot three times. The sailors dropped the pole and ran.

I looked back at Alan. He was standing over Mr. Shuan, his sword dripping with blood. Mr. Shuan was on his hands and knees. Someone outside the roundhouse grabbed him by his heels and pulled him out onto the deck. At that very moment, I saw the color go out of Mr. Shuan's face. He had died before my eyes.

For a few minutes it was quiet. "They are sure to attack again," I said.

"Aye." Alan grinned. "And this time they will have a better plan."

No sooner had he spoken than the second charge began. Alan stood in the open doorway, holding off a half dozen sailors.

Suddenly the glass skylight caved in. One of the sailors dropped through it. I didn't want to shoot a man point blank.

But he rose to his feet and grabbed me. Now I had no choice. I pulled the trigger. He gave out a loud groan and fell dead.

Seconds later, another sailor dropped through the broken skylight. This time I didn't think twice. I shot him too.

Alan's own fight looked hopeless. It was six against one. But he danced his way into the center of the group. His sword flashed like quicksilver. I heard one of the sailors cry out in pain. Then another. At last, they all turned and ran.

This time the battle was really over. Captain Hoseason came to the window and begged for a truce. Three men were dead and another badly wounded. The crew refused to fight anymore. The captain promised to put Alan and me safely ashore.

Alan was in high spirits. "What a

bonny fighter I am!" he crowed. He hugged me tight. "Oh, David, I love you like a brother."

Maybe I should have been sorry about the men I killed. Instead, I was almost as excited as Alan. We had won! It was thrilling just to be alive.

7

The Shipwreck

While the captain steered towards shore, Alan and I stayed in the roundhouse. Alan passed the time by telling me stories about the wild Highlanders.

Because I had fought by his side, he cut a silver button from his coat and gave it to me.

"Wherever you go in the Highlands, show this button," he said to me. "The friends of Alan Breck will come to your aid."

I told Alan about Mr. Campbell, the only person from my old life who had been good to me. Alan was not happy to hear of him. In the Highlands, Alan said, the Campbells and the Stewarts were enemies.

One of the Campbells, a man named Colin Roy of Glenure, had just become King George's agent in the Highlands, Alan explained. His job was to collect rent from the farmers. But the rebels had already taken the rent money in the name of the Stuarts. The farmers couldn't afford to pay twice. So Colin Roy was going to drive the poor farm families off their land.

"This Colin Roy is a red-haired man," said Alan. "He is known as the Red Fox."

Alan looked at me darkly. "We will never be free until his blood is on the hillside. If I have time, I may do a bit of fox hunting myself."

This talk struck me as foolish. If Colin Roy was killed, King George would send another man in his place. Surely, the Stuart cause was hopeless. But there was so much anger in Alan's voice that I knew I could not reason with him. So I kept silent.

While Alan told me tales of past Highland battles, our ship sailed into more rough weather. Soon Captain Hoseason came to the door.

"Can ye pilot a ship at all?" he asked Alan.

"What is this? A trick?" Alan asked back.

But it was no trick. The ship was running near the rocky Isle of Mull. There were hidden reefs all along the coast. Mr. Shuan, the navigator, was dead. The captain had no map and was terrified.

We went out on deck. Alan said he knew a little about the coastline. He did his best to set a course away from the reefs. Hugging the wind, the ship sheered to one side and then to the other.

After a while, it seemed the worst was behind us. "You saved the ship, sir," the captain told Alan.

But at that moment, the tide caught the *Covenant*. The ship spun around like a top. It crashed into a reef with such force that I was knocked off my feet. Seconds later, a huge wave tilted the ship onto her side, and I was thrown into the sea.

I went down twice. When I came up for the second time, the current had swept me far from the *Covenant*. I grabbed hold of a piece of floating timber and began kicking my way toward the shore.

An hour later, I was cast up onto a small island. I had swallowed a good bit of the sea. My legs felt like logs. But I dared not lie down to rest. It was a cold night. In my wet clothes I was in danger of freezing to death. So I walked the shore until dawn.

I have read many books about ship-wrecks. The survivors always seem to have tools and supplies to keep them alive. I had nothing. There was no sign of my shipmates. Even the money from Uncle Ebenezer was gone. It had fallen out of my pocket. Later I found three coins in the sand. The rest of the gold I never saw again.

My little island was separated from the

larger Isle of Mull by a deep creek. Across the water I could see the smoke from a chimney. But I was no swimmer.

For three days I slept in a crude shelter. Small shellfish clung to the rocks along the shore. I picked them off and ate them raw. I was so hungry that they tasted wonderful.

On the fourth day I saw two fishermen in a boat. I screamed for help. Instead of coming to rescue me, they laughed. One of them shouted at me. I could hardly hear him, but I made out the word "tide."

All at once I understood. I had been roaming the island for four days, but every time I came to the creek it was high tide. Now I waited for the tide to go out. Nothing was left of the creek but a trickle of water. I walked across to the Isle of Mull.

No wonder those fishermen had laughed! A lad who knew the ways of the sea would have been off the island in a few hours.

8

• •

The Murder of the Red Fox

The Isle of Mull was as bare as the place I had just left—all bogs, briar bushes, and rocks. I followed the chimney smoke that I had been watching for the last four days. Soon I reached the house of a poor farmer. Its single room was filled with black smoke from a peat fire.

The farmer told me that my shipmates

from the *Covenant* had been saved. One of them, the man with the fine clothes, had left a message for me. I was to follow him by way of the Torosay ferry.

I had heard frightening tales about the wild Highlanders, but this farmer was friendly. He fed me and gave me a place to sleep.

Others on the road to Torosay were not so kind. One man who offered to travel with me was blind. He said that he taught Bible classes to little children. But soon he began asking a lot of odd questions. How much money did I have with me? Was I armed?

Just then the man's coat fell open. I could see a pistol stuck in his belt. Was he planning to rob me? To be on the safe side, I lied and told him that I had a gun, too. I never thought a blind man could be a highway robber. But later I learned that's just what he was.

In four days of walking, I reached Torosay. There I took the ferry across the sound between the Isle of Mull and the mainland. I was heading into the part of the country where the Stewarts lived. Even the man who ran the ferry was related to the Stewarts. When I showed him Alan's silver button, he gave me directions to a place called Appin. There I would find the house of Alan's cousin, a man known as James of the Glens.

A passenger on the ferry told me that Colin Roy of Glenure had just arrived in Appin. He had brought English soldiers with him. They were to drive the farmers off the land.

"I feel sorry for the poor farmers," said the passenger. "But some of these Highlanders will stop at nothing. There will be shooting for sure. That Alan Breck is a tough customer."

I was surprised to hear my friend talked about this way. Perhaps it was true. But I had come to think that there was something fine about the bold Highlander. He was a brave man.

More ferries awaited me after Torosay. In this part of the country, fingers of the sea reached far into the mountains. Travel was difficult. But the wild landscape was beautiful.

Two days later I came to Linnhe Loch, the last stretch of open water on the way to Appin. The sea here was very deep and still. The mountains on either side were high, rough, and bare. They looked black in the shadow of the clouds. But where the sun shone on the mountainsides, little streams made them look laced with silver. Still, it was a hard land that Alan Breck loved.

I found a boatman to take me across the inlet to Appin. Just before we landed, I spotted a file of red-coated English soldiers marching along the shore. I could see that I was heading straight into trouble. After the boatman left me, I sat down on a rock to think things over.

Soon, four men on horseback came riding up the road. The man in the lead was tall and red-haired, with a lordly manner. I had no doubt that he was the Red Fox, Colin Roy. The second man must have been his servant. Behind them rode the sheriff's agent and a lawyer. They were coming to turn the farmers out of their homes.

The ferryman had warned me to hide

in the bushes if I met up with any of the king's men. But I was from the Lowlands, and I saw no reason to be afraid. Boldly, I stepped into the road. I asked for directions to the village where James of the Glens lived.

"What business do you have there?" the Red Fox asked. "Is James gathering his people?"

"I am neither his people, nor yours," I said bravely, "but an honest subject of King George who fears no man."

"Well said," the Fox replied. "But I warn you, I have twelve files of soldiers following me."

Suddenly there came a shot from high up on the hill behind me. The Red Fox fell off his horse onto the road. "Oh, I am dead!" he cried out.

Up on the hillside I saw a big man in a

black coat, carrying a long gun. "The murderer!" I shouted. "There he is! I see him!"

The man began to run, and I chased after him. Glancing back down the hill, I saw that the some of the redcoats had heard the shot and come running.

"A reward if you catch the boy!' the lawyer called out to them. "He is one of them!"

The soldiers were aiming their guns at me! My heart jumped into my mouth. At that moment, I heard a voice close by. "Duck in here," it ordered me.

It was my friend Alan. He was standing with a fishing rod, hidden among a clump of birch trees. "Come!" he said. And we took off.

We crawled on all fours through bushes of heather. But every so often

Alan stood up in plain sight, drawing the soldiers' fire. This went on for fifteen minutes.

At last, Alan clapped me on the shoulder. "Now," he said. "Do as I do and run for your life!"

9

****

We Flee the Highlands

I ran through trees and through heather, until my sides ached. Finally both of us fell on the ground in a woods, panting like dogs.

When I caught my breath, I said, "Alan, I like you very well. But this is where we go our separate ways. I'll have no part of a murder."

Alan swore that he had nothing to do

with the shooting. Still, I knew that he had helped the man in the black coat to get away.

"Why did you put us in danger for the sake of a killer?" I demanded.

Alan was surprised that I needed to ask. "Because you and I were innocent," he explained. "The innocent can at least expect their day in court. But the lad that did the shooting had no hope unless he got away."

It seemed to me that Alan's morals were tail-first. He would stand by his side even when it was in the wrong.

Alan explained that all Highlanders thought the same way. I realized his talk about the innocent having their day in court was just a grim joke. There was no hope of justice in a Highland court of law. The Stewarts and the Campbells hated each other too much.

"You Low Country folk have no notion of right and wrong," he told me. "A Campbell has been killed. And a Campbell jury must see that someone hangs for it, whether it's the right man or not. That's only fair."

This reasoning was so strange that it made me laugh.

Alan laughed too. But I could see that for once he was really afraid. "Take my word for it, Davie," he said. "We must flee to the Low Country."

I hated the thought of running like a common criminal. But I had no choice.

It was after nightfall when we reached the house of Alan's kinsman, James of the Glens. We were hoping he would help us. We found his place in an uproar. Servants carrying torches were racing about the grounds.

Rebel guns had been stored at James's

farm. Before the night was out, troops would be coming to search the house and barn. The servants were pulling the guns from their hiding places. Then they rushed off to bury them on a nearby hillside.

James himself was in a panic. "This has been a terrible accident!" he cried.

"Hoot!" said Alan. "Are you not thankful that Colin Roy is dead?"

"Not since he was killed here," said James. "We folk of Appin will have to pay for it." He looked darkly at Alan. "When they see your clothes, they will know you have been in France. You must bury them."

"Not my clothes!" Alan said. His fine blue coat was covered with mud. Still, Alan was too vain to give it up.

We could have used Alan's belt full of

gold coins to help us in our flight. But he had already turned the money over to another of the rebels. James of the Glens gave us swords, a bag of food, and a little money to help us get away.

I felt sorry for James. He'd had nothing to do with the murder of the Red Fox. But he would surely be blamed.

As for Alan, I wasn't sure if he was innocent or not. What was he doing up on that hillside with a fishing rod? There was no stream anywhere around.

But there was no time to ask questions. The soldiers were close behind us. So we set out. Sometimes we walked. Sometimes we ran.

When dawn broke, we found ourselves on the bank of a fast-moving river. "We've got to get across," said Alan. "We can't let ourselves be trapped here."

He ran down the bank to a spot where three rocks rose out of the racing water. The sight of the rapids made me feel sick to my stomach. But Alan had no pity.

"Which will it be, lad?" he said. "Hanging or drowning?"

Without warning, he leaped across the rapids onto the first rock. Then he leaped again. I swallowed hard and jumped after him.

On the other side of the river we came to a pair of tall rocks, twenty feet high. Alan began to climb, and I followed. On our third try, we finally made the top. There we found a bowl-shaped hiding place, just big enough for the two of us.

After we caught our breath, Alan began to tease me. "Not much of a jumper, lad, are you?"

I was sorry that I had let Alan see my

fear of the rapids. But Alan soon apologized for making fun of me.

"Oh well, I was worried last night, too," he said. "Even Alan Breck was moving a little faster than normal."

"A little faster!" I cried. "You were running for your life!"

But Alan just smiled. We were both too tired to talk anymore. Soon we both fell sound asleep.

At mid-morning, Alan nudged me awake. "Shhh!" he whispered. "You were snoring."

He pointed down below. The English soldiers had caught up with us. They had set up their camp just upstream. Their sentries were all around us. One was posted on a rock almost as tall as ours. If we raised our heads, he would surely see us.

We lay as still as we could. The day

turned warm, and the sun beat down on us. The rocks got so hot that they burned my hand when I touched them. Soon we felt like pancakes frying on a griddle. We were dizzy from hunger and thirst. I lay there thinking about the night of the shipwreck. Even freezing to death would be better than this!

When night fell, we decided to take our chances. "As well one death as another," said Alan. We shinnied down the side of the rocks and crept past the sentries.

That night we slept in a cave in the wild mountains. We hid there five days, eating trout from a nearby stream. Then we struck out to the east.

Our path led us across the moor. I had never seen such a wasteland. There was nothing but dead trees, heather bushes, and pools of black water for miles around.

At noon we lay down in some bushes to rest. Alan took the first watch. I promised to take the second. But when it was my turn, I couldn't keep my eyes open. I was too tired. And the sound of the bees buzzing in the heather made me even more sleepy.

Soon, I dozed off.

10
....
The Quarrel

When I opened my eyes, I saw we were
no longer alone on the moor. A group of
soldiers on horseback were heading our
way. They had spread out to search for us
among the tall heather.

I woke Alan. He frowned when he saw
the soldiers. But he didn't scold me.
"Now we will have to play at being
rabbits," he said. With that, he took off
on all fours.

For the rest of the day we crawled from one clump of bushes to another. My knees ached. My hands were torn and bloody. At nightfall I begged for a rest. The redcoats had stopped searching and were setting up camp for the night.

Alan was out of breath. But he was still as cheerful as ever. "No sleep tonight," he said. "We can't give up now, after all we've come through."

"Alan," I cried. "I want to keep going. But I can't. I'm just too weak."

"Well then, laddie," he said, "I'll have to carry you."

I felt ashamed. Alan had so much courage. I forced myself to go on.

The next morning we reached the edge of the moor. We were safe at last. Or so I thought. Suddenly four ragged men jumped out of the heather. Two of them pulled daggers and held them to our throats. I was so tired that I almost didn't mind being captured.

After a while, I heard Alan whispering in the Highlanders' language with one of the men. "These are Cluny MacPherson's followers," he told me. "We couldn't have fallen into better hands."

I had heard of Cluny MacPherson. Six years ago, he had been one of the leaders of the rebel army. Everyone thought that he had fled to France. I was amazed to learn that he was still in Scotland.

We found Cluny living in a strange house built of tree trunks and mud against the side of a steep cliff. It looked like a wasps' nest. Cluny had been in hiding so long that he was glad to have visitors, even wanted criminals like Alan and me.

Cluny gave us a good dinner. Then he pulled out a greasy deck of cards. He and Alan started to play. But I was brought up to think that gambling was wrong. So I stretched out on a bed of heather and went to sleep.

The game went on for many hours. Once, I awoke and saw a huge pile of gold coins by my friend's place. But Alan's luck changed. By the time I woke up again, he had lost all his money and my few coins as well.

We had been counting on that money. We needed it to pay a boatman to take us back to the Lowlands. We might soon have a chance to buy food, too. How could Alan be so reckless? Lucky for us, Cluny MacPherson insisted on giving me back what Alan had lost.

After we left Cluny's hideout, the

going was not so hard. The soldiers were still searching for us. But now that we were off the moor, they had lost our trail.

It was a good thing, too. The fever I caught on the *Covenant* had come back. Every day it got worse. My head ached. I grew so weak I could hardly walk.

In my misery, my head filled with angry thoughts. It was Alan's fault that we were being hunted like common criminals. He had put us both in danger by refusing to get rid of his fancy clothes. And he had gambled with my money!

Alan said he was sorry. But I didn't believe him. He acted as if our flight were a great adventure. As we walked along, he sang Stuart songs. And he made bad jokes about King George and the Campbells. Now that there were no soldiers hot on our trail, he seemed to want to pick a fight with me. I began to think that Alan was acting like a spoiled child.

Finally I could stand no more. "Mr. Stewart," I said. "You are older than I am and should know your manners. From now on, watch what you say about my king."

Alan was taken by surprise. "David," he said. "Do you mean to insult me? I am a Stewart—"

"I know all about your people," I shot back. "They have been beaten by King George's army many times. And from what I saw, some of them could use a good bath, too."

"Davie, say no more," Alan begged. "Some words cannot be forgotten."

I was still wearing the sword that James of the Glens had given me. I reached for it. "That's all right," I said. "I am ready to fight you."

Alan drew his sword. But his face had gone white. "David, you wouldn't have a chance. I can't fight you. It would be as good as murder."

I was too angry to listen. "You should have thought of that before." I made a thrust with my sword.

"Nay, nay. I can't fight you." Alan dropped his weapon. He stood there waiting for me to strike him.

When I saw that, the anger rushed out of me. What had I been thinking of? I almost stabbed my best friend!

At that moment, I felt a sharp pain in my side. I must have fainted. When I came to, I knew I was too sick to go on.

"Help me, Alan," I begged, "or I'm done for."

Another man would have refused to help. I had behaved badly. Very badly. But Alan would never leave a friend in need, even to save his own life. He could see that I would die without a doctor. So he put his arm around me and helped me walk.

In this way Alan led me down out of the hills. When we found a house, he knocked on the door and asked the family to help me.

This was the bravest thing I had ever seen Alan do. The people who lived in the house might be Whigs. If they were loyal to King George, they would turn us over to the army. Alan was willing to take that chance to save my life.

11

⋅⋅⋅⋅⋅⋅⋅⋅⋅⋅⋅⋅⋅⋅⋅⋅⋅⋅⋅⋅⋅⋅⋅⋅⋅⋅⋅⋅⋅⋅⋅

I Come Into My Fortune

We were in luck. The house belonged to a family named Maclaren who were on the side of the Stuarts. They nursed me back to health and hid us both from the soldiers.

At last, the worst of our journey was behind us. A few days after leaving the Maclarens, we reached Queen's Ferry. Now that we were back in the Lowlands, we really did need money. Alan would have to flee the country.

Luckily, no one in the Highlands had known my full name. I was safe. But I would have to get on with my life.

I decided to call on Mr. Rankeillor. He may have been Uncle Ebenezer's lawyer, but everyone said he was an honest man.

Rankeillor was amazed to see me alive. "Your friend Parson Campbell has been looking for you," he said. "But Captain Hoseason swore you were dead. Drowned at sea."

At long last, I learned the truth about my family. "It all goes back to a love affair," the lawyer told me.

Just as I had thought, my father was older than Uncle Ebenezer. As young men, the brothers fell in love with the same girl. The girl chose my father. But

Uncle made so much trouble that my father finally left home. He and his sweetheart ran off to Essendean, where I was born.

But when my father disappeared, people thought that Uncle had murdered him. They would have nothing to do with Ebenezer. He became an unhappy miser.

"By rights, the estate is yours," Rankeillor said, stroking his chin. "But what now? Lawsuits are costly."

Perhaps I had been too long with Alan. I decided not to count on the law. I would use my wits to get justice. I already had a plan in mind.

The next morning, the lawyer, his clerk, and I set out for Shaws. Alan came with us. Poor Mr. Rankeillor was very nervous about being in the company of an outlaw rebel. He pretended not to know who Alan was.

When we reached the house of Shaws, Alan knocked on the door while the rest of us hid nearby. Alan told my uncle a fantastic story. He said his family had rescued me from the wreck of the *Covenant* and was holding me for ransom.

"If ye like the lad, ye will pay to have him back," said Alan. "And if ye do not want him back, ye may pay a pretty penny to see that he never returns."

Uncle pretended to be shocked. But he knew a good bargain when he heard one. He told Alan he didn't want me killed, just held prisoner.

Alan pretended to be thinking about how much money to ask for. "I want the same price you paid Hoseason for the kidnapping," he said.

"It's a lie!" cried Uncle. "The boy was never kidnapped!"

"It's no good denying it," Alan said. "Hoseason and I are in this together. I know everything."

At that, my uncle broke down and admitted the truth. Then Mr. Rankeillor stepped out of hiding and threatened to have him arrested.

In the end, Uncle accepted our terms. He would be allowed to stay at Shaws as long as he lived. But he would pay me two-thirds of his income.

I had come into my fortune at last.

Now I was a rich man. But I had not forgotten my friends in the Highlands. Poor James of the Glens had been arrested for Colin Roy's murder. Mr. Rankeillor told me not to get involved in a Highland quarrel. But I knew that

James was innocent. So I went to the king's lawyer and offered to testify for him.

As for Alan, it was time for him to go back into hiding. I paid some money to a man named Stewart, who would help him escape to France.

We parted with a simple handshake. But when he was gone, I felt so lost and lonesome that I wanted to cry. Alan Breck had been a great friend to me. But he was also an outlaw. I felt sure that we would never meet again.

Robert Louis Stevenson was born in Scotland in 1850. He was sick most of his life. Because he thought that a change in climate would improve his health, Stevenson traveled a great deal—to Europe, the United States, and the South Seas. But his illnesses did not keep him from his greatest loves—reading and writing. He wrote constantly and became one of the most popular writers of his time.

Stevenson is best known for writing *Treasure Island*, *The Strange Case of Dr. Jekyll and Mr. Hyde*, and *Kidnapped*. He also wrote *A Child's Garden of Verses*, a collection of poetry for children.

Robert Louis Stevenson died on the South Sea island of Samoa at the age of forty-four.

Lisa Norby has written several other books, including the Bullseye Step into Classics adaptation of *Treasure Island*. When not writing, she loves to travel. She lives in Brooklyn, New York.